Look for these

ROTTEN SCHOOL
books, too!

The Big
Blueberry
Barf~Off!

The Good, the Bad
and the Very Slimy

ROTTEN SCHOOL

The Great Smelling Bee

R.L. STINE

Illustrations by Trip Park

SCHOLASTIC INC.

New York Toronto London Auckland Sydney
Mexico City New Delhi Hong Kong Buenos Aires

To Sumner
–TP

ISBN 0-439-82232-7

12 11 10 9 8 7 6 5 4 3 2   6 7 8 9 10 11/0

Printed in the U.S.A.   23

First Scholastic printing, January 2006

Cover and interior design by mjcdesign

CONTENTS

MORNING ANNOUNCEMENTS

Good morning, everyone. This is Headmaster Upchuck. I'd like all of you Rotten Students to settle down now so I can read the Morning Announcements.

As you know, I read important news over the loudspeaker every morning. It's my way of saying good morning to you all without having to leave my office and see your grinning faces.

Ow! That really hurt my ears!

Doesn't anybody know how to stop that horrible squealing?

OWW!

I hope you can hear me. Here are today's Morning Announcements. . . .

Tryouts for the Armpit Band will be held in the second-floor boys' locker room. If you play either one or both armpits, you are urged to try out. Don't come just to be funny. You *must* be serious about playing the armpit.

Any student who ate the pigeon stew in Ms. Sally Monella's fourth-period cooking class—please stop by the nurse's office this morning to have your stomach pumped.

Attention art students. Third grader Billy Bob Heffernan will be showing off his new tattoos in the gym after school.

There is a mistake on the posters you see around campus. We are inviting all students to enter the SPELLING Bee. Not SMELLING Bee. The Smelling Bee—I mean, *Spelling* Bee—will be held next Friday. Warning: All the words will be three-letter words— so it will be hard! But we want all good smellers to join in. Did I say smellers? I meant spellers.

Finally, bathroom privileges for fourth graders will be suspended for the rest of the month.

Chapter 1

DO I LOOK TENSE?

I'm Bernie Bridges, and I usually walk around with a dazzling smile. Ask anyone. When I smile, it's sunshine. *Sunshine!* Not to mention my adorable dimples.

But today I wasn't smiling. Today my handsome forehead was wrinkled from heavy thoughts. Behind my glasses, my big brown eyes darted from side to side.

Tense? Was I tense?

Does a lizard change its spots?

Dude, I was tense. I had a problem.

Yesterday

Today

A problem that could get me into major trouble. A problem that could get me booted out of school.

You probably don't have this kind of problem. Because you go home every day.

But I live at the Rotten School. It's a boarding school. That means I don't go home. I live here in a dorm with a bunch of other guys.

Actually, we live in an old house called Rotten House. A whole bunch of fourth and fifth graders live here, and we love it.

My friends and I claimed the third floor, because it's good for dropping things out the window on people.

Mrs. Heinie says it's against school rules to drop things on people. She knows all the rules. She's always sniffing around, snooping on us, telling us the rules we are breaking.

But that's her job. She is our dorm mother. She is in charge of all us guys who live in Rotten House, and she is our fourth-grade core teacher.

Mrs. Heinie has her own apartment in the attic. We think she has spy cameras up there. Because she always knows when we're dropping things out the window on people.

Mrs. Heinie is very nearsighted. Her glasses are as thick as ice cubes.

But she still knows *everything*!

That's why I'm afraid she's going to discover my secret. And then I'm DOOMED.

How did I get in this mess?

Well...that's a whole other chapter.

Chapter 2

A WHOLE OTHER CHAPTER

The Whole Other Chapter began this morning.

I was smiling. Innocent. Happy. Did I have a care in the world?

I don't think so.

My faithful friend Belzer carried my breakfast in on a tray. He brings me breakfast in bed every morning.

Good kid, Belzer.

It took me a long time to train him. But it was worth it.

Belzer is a chubby guy with red hair and freckles. This morning he was wearing his Rotten School blazer. We all have to wear the school uniform.

But under his blazer, Belzer was wearing a white T-shirt with bright blue letters across the front. The T-shirt said: I NEED A TUTOR.

Sad, huh?

He wears these loser T-shirts. But, hey—I always tell him he's looking good. I like to keep my guys happy.

Belzer poured my orange juice for me. Then he went across the hall to his room.

I nibbled on a few things…eggs, bacon, blueberry muffins, hash brown potatoes, flapjacks, cornflakes with bananas, and apple cobbler.

All part of a healthy breakfast—right?

After I swallowed the last crumb of cobbler, I did the Official Rotten School Burp for a few minutes.

Burp!

Then I climbed out of bed and put on my school uniform.

I practiced smiling in the mirror for a while. "Bernie, those dimples are *killer*!"

Happy. Innocent. Carefree.

And then the box arrived.

Belzer staggered into my room, carrying a HUGE wooden crate in both arms. "Big B, this just came for you," he said. "I…I carried it up three flights of stairs." He let out a groan. "Heavy," he muttered. "Heavy." His knees buckled, and he fell to the floor.

"Why don't you set it down?" I asked.

"Oh. Good thinking." Belzer dropped the crate. Then he sprawled facedown on the floor, gasping for breath.

My two best buddies, Feenman and Crench, walked into the room.

Feenman and Crench are tall and lean and goofy looking. But they are serious dudes. Serious about having fun twenty-four hours a day.

Feenman has a strange hobby. He likes to paint things red when no one is looking. And Crench's hobby? Making funny noises with balloons.

Good guys.

Belzer, Feenman, and Crench are crammed into

10

the tiny room across from me. They insisted I take the big room for myself. They knew I need my own space. Lots of quiet so I can plan and scheme.

"What's up with the box?" Feenman asked.

I helped pull Belzer to his feet. "Probably a gift from one of my admirers," I said. "Maybe the teachers all chipped in to buy me something special. You know. To thank me just for being me."

Crench walked around the crate. "The box is as big as our room," he said. "After you empty it, could I live in the box, Bernie? *Could* I?"

"Don't be bitter," I said. I studied the wooden crate. "Maybe April-May June sent me a big box of chocolates."

April-May June is the coolest, hottest, blondest, snobbiest girl in the fourth grade. "It's about time she started to notice me," I said. I patted the side of the box. "Think she sent me flowers?"

"Bernie, the box is from your parents," Feenman said. "Look at the writing on the side. It says 'Mr. and Mrs. Benny Bridges.'"

"My parents sent this box?" I felt a little pang in my heart, a moment of sadness. I love living at the

Rotten School, but sometimes I miss my parents.

They are travel writers, so they travel all the time. That's why they send me to boarding school. We keep in touch by e-mail and cell phone. I get to tell them how great I'm doing and how everyone thinks I'm awesome.

But it isn't the same as telling them in person.

I studied the box. "A present from my parents… hmmm." What could it be?

Maybe it's a car, I thought. They know I *hate* walking to class. No. Maybe it's a PlayStation with a few hundred games. They know I need time off. I've been studying way too hard.

No. Suddenly, I knew.

"Dudes, why aren't you cheering?" I cried. "Why aren't you celebrating? Come on—hurry. Go crazy. Go crazy!"

They stared at me.

"Don't you know this is our lucky day?" I said. "Don't you know what's in the box? It's the wide-screen TV I've been begging for!"

"Yes!" Belzer shouted, pumping his fists in the air. "Sweet!"

"I finally convinced my parents that TV is educational," I said. "I said I need to watch *Fear Factor* every week to learn what *not* to do!"

"Sweet!" Belzer cried again. He slapped me a high five. "Our own widescreen TV!" We touched knuckles. Then we did the secret Rotten House Handshake.

"But, Bernie," Feenman said. He pulled me to the back of the crate. "If it's a TV, what's up with the air holes in the box?"

"Huh? Air holes?"

I stared at the round holes cut into the crate. And then all four of us heard a scratching sound. Something scratching the inside of the crate.

"It's ALIVE!" Crench screamed. "The TV is ALIVE!"

"It's alive!
It's alive!"

Chapter 3

WHAT STINKS?

We heard more scratching sounds, and then a loud *squaaaawk*. Something was definitely alive in there. We had to get that box open—fast!

Belzer found tools in the basement. They went to work, prying open the lid. Feenman and Crench used crowbars. Belzer used a claw hammer. I did the most important job: I cheered them on. "Let's go, dudes! Good job! Good job!"

It meant a lot to them.

A few minutes later, the lid popped up, and the front of the box fell to the floor with a crash. My

mouth dropped open as I stared in disbelief at two
animals.

A dog and a parrot.

MY dog and MY parrot!

"My pets!" I cried.
I dove forward and
dropped to the
floor of the crate
to hug my fat,
sloppy bulldog.

Lippy, my
beautiful
green parrot,
squawked.
"Go *bite a*
WALNUT!"

Isn't he
sweet? Who
taught him
to say that?
Was it me?

"Go *bite a*
WALNUT!"

19

Ha-ha. He cracks me up.

I hugged my dog. "Good to see you, fella!"

He snorted hello and drooled drippy stuff all over the front of my school blazer.

Belzer stuck his head into the crate. "But, Bernie, where's the TV?"

"There's no TV. It's my pets from home!" I cried. "I guess they missed me so much, Mom and Dad mailed them to school."

I felt so happy. I'd really missed my pets. And now here they were. Awesome!

I jumped up and smoothed Lippy's feathers. "Are you a good boy, Lippy?" I whispered to the parrot. "Are you a pretty boy?"

"*Eat birdseed and CHOKE!*" Lippy squawked.

Isn't he *cute*?

Feenman and Crench dropped down on their knees and started to pet my big bulldog. We heard a loud

The dog let out a moan. They suddenly stopped petting him.

Feenman made a horrified face. "Ooh, what STINKS?" he gasped.

"The dog!" Crench cried. "Bernie—your dog—he STINKS! Oh, it's bad. It's BAD!"

"Hold your breath," I said. "It'll go away in a minute or two."

"I *am* holding my breath!" Belzer cried. "It doesn't help!" The poor guy had tears running down his cheeks. He staggered away, choking, his fingers pressed to his nose.

"Oh, man, that's BAD!" Feenman groaned.

Crench dove for the window, pulled it open, and stuck his head outside.

"Bernie, what's your dog's name?" Feenman asked.

"Gassy," I said.

Feenman nodded. "Good name."

Chapter 4

PARROT PLOP

Feenman and Crench both hung their heads out the window, breathing fresh air. The smell faded away in a couple of minutes. I told them it would.

I hoisted Gassy up and carried the big sweetie to my bed. He pushed his snout under my pillow and fell asleep with a sigh.

Lippy stood on his metal perch, clucking softly to himself. I lifted the perch from the box and set it up in the corner by the bed.

I felt so happy to have my pets with me. I didn't stop to think about the trouble I was in.

"Hey, look—" Crench cried. He pointed to the floor of the crate. "Big B, there's a note from your parents in the box."

He reached down and pulled up a sheet of paper. "Hey, what's this green gloppy stuff all over it?" Crench switched the paper to his left hand. His right hand was covered in green-and-yellow goop.

Feenman laughed. "It's bird doo!"

"Huh?" Crench smelled his hand. "Whoa." He looked from hand to hand. They were both covered in the thick, sticky glop.

Feenman tossed back his head and let out a long hee-haw. "Bird plop alert!" he shouted.

Crench moved fast. "Shake hands," he said. He grabbed Feenman's hand and shook it.

"Yuccck." Feenman made a sick face. Now he had bird plop oozing over his hand.

Crench wiped both of his hands on Feenman's jacket sleeve. "All clean," he said, holding up his hands.

"You jerk!" Feenman cried. He wiped his hand across Crench's cheek. Now Crench had bird doo smeared all over his face.

26

He raised the gloppy letter, pushed it into Feenman's face, and wiped it around. Feenman angrily grabbed the letter, and it ripped into two pieces. He stuffed the gloppy pieces into Crench's mouth.

What did I tell you? These are fun-loving dudes!

"Uh...guys," I said. "Guys, what does the letter say?"

They turned to me. They were both covered in bird plop. Green-and-yellow goop on their faces, their hands, their school uniforms. Crench was wiping it off his lips.

"I'll try to read it," Feenman said. He pulled the gloppy letter from Crench's mouth. He put the two pieces together. "Uh...it says your parents have to go away for a long time, and they couldn't find anyone to take care of your pets. If you don't take Gassy, he'll have to go to the pound. And the parrot will have to go to a zoo."

"No way!" I cried. "I'll take care of them. They're my sweeties!"

"But, Bernie, you can't," Crench said, spitting bird doo off his lips. "You'll be in major trouble."

27

I stared at him. "Huh? Me?"

He wiped green glop from his hair. "Yeah. You know the school rule: No Pets Allowed."

Oh, wow. No Pets Allowed.

A chill ran down my back. Crench was right. No Pets Allowed.

"If Mrs. Heinie catches you…," Crench said. He made a slicing motion across his neck. "You're dead meat."

Crench was right again. If Mrs. Heinie found out I was hiding my animals in my room—and told Headmaster Upchuck—it would be "Bye-bye, Bernie."

I'm in major trouble, I thought. *Unless I can find a way to hide Lippy and Gassy, I'll be on the next bus home.*

I sat down on my bed beside my snoring bulldog and started to think. I had to protect my pets. But how could I hide them? How?

Feenman and Crench dragged the crate from my room. Then they headed for the showers.

And exactly two seconds later, I heard the click of Mrs. Heinie's shoes in the hall. She was heading for my room!

"Quiet, Lippy," I whispered. "Don't make a sound!"

"*Go bite a WALNUT!*" Lippy squawked.

Mrs. Heinie stepped in and squinted at me through her thick glasses. "Bernie, who were you talking to?" she asked.

Chapter 5

BUSTED!

"Uh…who was I talking to? Myself," I said. "I'm giving myself a pep talk. You know. To be a better student." I stood up and shook her hand. "You've inspired me, Mrs. Heinie. You've inspired me to work harder. To be an even greater person than I am."

She gave me a weak smile. "That's very nice, Bernie."

"BEAK me!" Lippy squawked. "BEAK me!"

Mrs. Heinie squinted at me again. "What did you say?"

"Just clearing my throat," I said.

30

She gazed past me to the bird stand, and her mouth dropped open. "Oh, my! Is that a parrot? A parrot in the dorm?"

I turned. "You mean that new throw pillow? Isn't that nice? My mom sent that pillow to me from home. It *does* look a little like a bird, doesn't it!"

"*Beak me! BEAK me!*" Lippy cried.

"BEAK me."

Mrs. Heinie's smile faded. She narrowed her eyes at me. "Bernie, you know the rules about pets, don't you? Is that a *dog* lying on your bed? Oh, my! Oh, my!"

"Dog? Where? You mean that bag of laundry?"

"Let me take a closer look," Mrs. Heinie said. "Bernie, you know the rules. If you have pets in the dorm, I have to take you to Headmaster Upchuck. He will jump for joy. He'll be so happy! He'll have a reason to send you home."

"You mean Headmaster Upchuck doesn't *like* me?" I asked innocently.

"He hates your guts," she said. "Now let me take a close look at what you've got here."

Uh-oh. *No way* I can let her take a closer look.

"Mrs. H., you have a smear on your glasses," I said. "Let me clean them for you." I took her glasses and very carefully smeared my thumbs all over the lenses. Then I handed them back to her. "There. That should be better," I said.

She blinked several times.

"Birdseed for brains!" Lippy squawked.

"I can't see a thing," Mrs. Heinie said, blinking behind the smeared eyeglasses.

"You look awesome today, Mrs. H.," I said. "Did you do something new with your hair?"

"No, I didn't."

"Beak me! BEAK me!"

Mrs. Heinie gazed blindly around. "Bernie, where is that bird?"

"Bird? I don't hear a bird," I said. "I know you've changed your hair. You look ten years younger. Really."

"Eat feathers and DIE!"

Mrs. Heinie pulled off the glasses. Then she put them back on. She stared right at Gassy. But her glasses were totally smeared.

I heard a loud

BRAAAAT!

Mrs. Heinie started to say something. Her mouth opened wide. She let out a gasp. "That odor! It's making me *sick!*" she cried. "Bernie—what is that *stink?*"

Gassy had performed his special trick once again.

Think fast, Bernie. Think fast, dude.

"Uh…it must be the blueberries from my pancakes," I said, pointing to my breakfast tray. "I think they were a little too ripe."

Mrs. Heinie had her fingers pinched over her nose. "It doesn't smell like blueberries to me," she said. "Are you having stomach problems?"

She gazed at my breakfast tray. "Bernie, why are you eating breakfast in your room? Why aren't you in the dining hall?"

I pulled out a Kleenex. "I have the sniffles this morning," I said. "I didn't want to infect everyone else."

Mrs. Heinie gave me a warm smile. "That's very considerate of you."

I lowered my head humbly. "I try to set a good example for others," I said.

"*BEAK me!*" Lippy squawked. "*Eat birdseed and DIE!*"

34

Chapter 6

MY RAFFLE SURPRISE

Whoa. That was a close one.

An ordinary kid would be packing his bags right now. But not Bernie B.

Did you see the master at work? When it comes to Mrs. Heinie's glasses, I've got Thumbs of Steel.

But I don't think Mrs. Heinie was fooled. She's a smart cookie. She said she'd be keeping a close eye on my room. I didn't like the sound of that.

But what could I do? I had to protect my pets. They're not pets to me. They're like my two brothers. Only featherier and smellier.

I needed a plan. I knew I could cover Lippy's perch. That always shuts him up for a little while. But how could I hide Gassy?

I was late for class. I hid both pets in the dorm Study Hall room. I knew they'd be safe. No one *ever* goes in there.

A few minutes later, my brain was whirring in high gear as I made my way downstairs.

I passed the Common Room. That's our living room. "Yo—Billy!" I said, and waved to my friend Billy the Brain. He was hunched over a table, reading a manga comic book.

Why do we call him the Brain? Because—duh—he's the fourth-grade class brain. The kid has a solid C-minus average. Best in the school!

How does he do it? He works hard for it. Hey, this brainiac studies almost *half an hour* every night.

I stepped out the front door and down the steps. Then I started to jog across the Great Lawn to my first class.

It was a sunny day. The grass sparkled. The sky was cloudless and blue. My empty backpack bounced on my back. Belzer was carrying all of my books for me.

Up ahead, I saw Feenman and Crench walking to the School House. That's what we call our classroom building. I hurried to catch up to them. "You still have a little green stuff in your nose," I told Crench.

He wiped it out with his finger. "What did you do with your pets, Bernie?"

"They're safe," I said. "I hid them in a room that no one ever uses."

"You mean the Study Hall?"

"Right," I said. "Now let's get to business, dudes. Give me the report. How are the raffle tickets selling?"

Crench shook his head. "Not well."

"They're not selling at all," Feenman said.

My heart skipped a beat. "You mean you've only sold a hundred tickets? Two hundred?" I asked.

"We haven't sold any," Feenman said. "Kids don't want to buy two-dollar raffle tickets from you."

"Whoa." My mouth dropped open. "But it's for such a good cause," I said. "Aren't we tired of soggy pizza? Every dollar goes to buying a new pizza oven for the Dining Hall. Just think of it, dudes. In a few weeks, our pizza will be crisp! Crisp and flaky! Look at me—I'm drooling. I'm *drooling* already!"

Feenman shook his head. "Everyone thinks you're just going to keep the money, Bernie. Like the last two raffles."

"That's crazy," I said. "Mrs. Heinie asked me to hold this raffle. She put me in charge. I can't let her down, guys. We have to sell those tickets."

Crench squinted at me. "*Mrs. Heinie* asked you to hold this raffle?"

"Yes," I said. "Of course, she was talking in her sleep. But that counts. That counts!"

"But, Bernie," Crench said, "kids want to know what the prize is. You can't have a raffle without a prize."

"There's going to be an *awesome* prize," I said. "I just haven't thought of it yet. Tell them it's a *secret* prize! The prize is so totally *outstanding*, I have to keep it a secret."

My two buddies shrugged their shoulders. "They won't buy, Bernie," Crench said. "Not even the second graders. Feenman and I think you should give up."

"Give up?" I cried. I jumped in front of them. "Give up? Give up and eat gummy pizza for the rest of the year? I'd rather starve!"

"But, Bernie—" Feenman started.

"Dudes—whoa. Hold on," I said. "Did you sell any tickets to Sherman?"

Sherman Oaks is the spoiled, rich kid who lives in the dorm across from us, the dorm we all hate. It's called Nyce House.

"No. Sherman Oaks wouldn't buy any," Feenman said. "Sherman said he *likes* soggy pizza. He said he pays extra for soggy crust."

"He would," I muttered. "Well, there he is now." I pointed. "Now take a lesson, guys. Watch Bernie go to work. Hide behind that tree and watch how it's done."

Feenman grabbed my arm. "He won't buy, Bernie. Sherman won't buy a raffle ticket if he doesn't know the prize."

"Just watch," I said. "I'll make Sherman *beg* me to sell him some raffle tickets! He'll *beg*!"

I rubbed my hands together, thinking about how I'd handle Sherman Oaks.

"Hey, Sherman!" I shouted. "Sherman! Wait up!"

Chapter 7

SHERMAN OAKS HAS A PET

Sherman turned and flashed me his perfect, gleaming smile. I gazed at the smooth, blond hair, his crisply starched school uniform, his deep tan, his sparkling blue eyes, the sneer on his thin lips.

He wore an ostrich-skin backpack with the price tag still on it—$300. He had a platinum iPod in his blazer pocket.

Still grinning at me, he pulled off the ear pieces. "Bernie," he said, "I hear you're hiding two pets in your dorm room."

GAAACK.

My pets arrived half an hour ago! How did he find out? How did my biggest *enemy* on earth find out my biggest secret?

I grabbed my head. I felt dizzy. My stomach rocked. And rolled. I was sick. SICK!

"Pets? I don't know what you're talking about," I said. "What is up with all these *false rumors* about me?"

Sherman's ugly grin grew wider. "In Nyce House, we like to follow the rules," he said. "It keeps us out of trouble. Know what I mean?"

Was he threatening me? Was he threatening to tell Headmaster Upchuck about my pets?

Sherman stuck out his hand to shake hands. "I just want to say good-bye, Bernie. This might be the last time I see you. I mean, if I should *accidentally* tell Headmaster Upchuck about your pets..."

Uh-oh. He *was* threatening me!

"Why would I have pets?" I said. "I'm allergic to them. Just the *word* makes me itch. Look. Look. Don't *say* that word! I'm itching all over." I went into a scratching fit, scratching every part of my body.

"You need a pet like mine, Bernie," Sherman said. He pointed to a hunk of shiny metal at his feet.

"I don't believe this," I said. "Now you've got your own personal trash can!"

"It's a digital robot pet," Sherman said. "It cost

one thousand dollars. My parents sent it to me because they think they can buy my love with expensive, shiny toys."

I stared at the thing. It was kinda shaped like a cat.

"Watch this," Sherman said. He took out a thin remote controller and aimed it at the metal pet. "Say hello, Money. Say hello to Bernie."

"*Money?*" I said. "You named your pet *Money?*"

"Yeah. Cute name, isn't it?" Sherman pushed some buttons on the controller. "Say hello, Money."

The little robot squeaked, "*Mee-ow. Mee-ow.*"

Sherman laughed. "Isn't that totally fabulous? Now watch this." He pushed more buttons.

The robot pet ran around the grass in a big circle. Then it rolled over. Then it jumped into the air a few times and wagged its metal tail.

Sherman laughed. He got down on his knees to pet the thing. "Good boy! Good, Money! Good!" He looked up at me. "See? This pet won't get me in trouble."

"Let me try it," I said. I took the remote from him. I pushed a few buttons.

The metal cat grabbed Sherman's face with its paws, latched on tight, and began to squeeze.

"Oww! Bernie! Stop it!" he screamed. "Stop it! Ow! It's *hurting* me!"

I stared at the controller. "I'm just no good at these things," I said. "How do you work it? I can't ever figure these things out."

"Stop it! Get it OFF me!" Sherman howled.

"It's so confusing," I said, shaking my head. "So many buttons. Do I push the blue ones or the red ones?"

"Owww! It's squeezing my face! Make it *stop*!"

I pushed a yellow button. The robot cat coughed up a metal hairball into Sherman's face.

"OW! OWWWW!

OW! OWWWW!"

"It's SQUEEZING my beautiful face!" he wailed. Should I give the guy a break?

44

Chapter 8

My Lucky Day

Hey, Bernie B. is a good guy. Of *course* I gave him a break.

A few minutes later, I made the tin cat open its paws. "So sorry, dude," I said. "I just can't ever work these things."

Sherman staggered to his feet. His cheeks were bright purple. "Thanks, Bernie. That was a close one," he said. He picked up the robot cat and shook it hard. "Bad boy! Bad boy!" he scolded. "No fresh batteries for you tonight." Sherman turned to me. "He likes it when I change his batteries."

46

"Glad I could rescue you," I said. "This *is* my lucky day, after all."

Sherman squinted his sky blue eyes at me. "Huh? Your lucky day?"

I nodded. "Yeah, dude. It's my lucky day." I pulled a bunch of raffle tickets from my pocket. "Check these out. Pizza oven raffle tickets. I bought the last ten tickets."

Sherman stared at the tickets in my fist. "You bought the last ten tickets?"

"I have the last ten raffle tickets. And I wouldn't sell them to anyone."

I waved them slowly in front of his face.

Sherman's mouth fell open, and he started to drool. "The last ten? You're serious? And you rigged the raffle, didn't you, Bernie? It's fixed, right? You made sure you have the winning ticket."

I grinned at him. "Would I do that? That would be cheating. You don't think I'm a cheater, *do* you, Sherman?" I waved the tickets in front of his face some more.

"I'll buy 'em off you, Bernie. How much? How much?"

"Not selling," I said. "Why would I sell the last ten tickets?"

Drool ran down Sherman's chin. His eyes bulged. He was breathing hard. "How much, Bernie? Come on. How about two bucks? I'll give you two bucks each for them."

He grabbed for the tickets. I swung them away from him.

"Oh, no," I said. "You want them too badly, Sherman. You *know* I have a winner here—don't you! You're trying to cheat me. Play fair, Sherman. Play fair!"

"Okay," he said. "Four dollars. Four dollars each. What do you say, Bernie? Four dollars."

I pretended to think about it. I rubbed my chin and shut my eyes. "Okay," I said finally. "It breaks my heart, but...four dollars each."

"Thank you! Thank you!"

Sherman cried. He handed me a wad of dollar bills, and I gave him the tickets. "Wow! The last ten tickets!" he said. "Thank you!" He picked up his robot cat and ran off to class.

I watched him go. Then I counted the money. Forty big ones.

I should have felt happy. The *master* had struck again!

But I was too worried to enjoy the money. Sherman knew about my pets. What if he squealed to Headmaster Upchuck?

I had to do something to hide them. And I had to act fast!

Chapter 9

SHERMAN SQUEALS

I caught up to Feenman and Crench. "Sherman was too easy. Too easy!" I said. I waved the wad of dollar bills in front of their noses.

Their tongues fell out of their mouths, and they started to pant.

"But, dudes, I've got a big problem," I said. "Mrs. H. almost busted me. She almost saw Lippy and Gassy. And Sherman Oaks knows about them. I'm afraid he'll tell Headmaster Upchuck."

I wiped the sweat off my forehead with a dollar bill. "If we don't find a better way to hide Gassy, I'll be waving bye-bye to you guys on the next bus."

"Bernie, that dog *stinks!*" Feenman said.

"Feenman, you don't smell that good yourself," I replied.

"I've got it! Maybe we could dress the dog up," Crench said. "Disguise him. You know. Maybe make him look like a cat."

"Like a *cat?*" I cried. "What good would that do? How would that help me with Mrs. Heinie?"

Crench scratched his chin. "Well…if she thinks the dog is a cat, it might confuse her."

I patted Crench on the head. "How many times have I told you not to think before noon? It puts a terrible strain on your brain."

"Sorry, Bernie."

We passed under a clump of apple trees. Up ahead stood a tall, old, brick building. Long vines of poison ivy clung to its walls. This was the School House, where all the classes are held.

I slipped into class just as the bell rang. Mrs. Heinie sat at her desk, cleaning her glasses.

I slid into my desk between Feenman and Crench. Headmaster Upchuck's voice came on the loudspeaker. The speaker squealed and whistled. It was hard to hear.

"I have two special announcements," the Headmaster said. "First, one of our lunchroom ladies is missing a leg. If you are the one who took it, you know who you are. Please return it to the kitchen, and no questions will be asked."

A lot of kids giggled at that one.

"Second," Upchuck continued, "twelve students signed up for the Smelling Bee. I must repeat—it is NOT a Smelling Bee. These students are very, very mixed up.

"So far," he said, "*no one* has signed up for the Spelling Bee. So we are going to make it a little easier. Only *two*-letter words will be used. I hope you will all enter the contest now. Thank you."

Mrs. Heinie stood up at the front of the classroom. The light reflected off her glasses. "Today, I thought we'd have a little fun and talk about state capitals," she said.

Everyone groaned.

Feenman had his head down on his desk. He was already sound asleep.

"Does anyone know the capital of South Dakota?" Mrs. Heinie asked.

No hands went up.

"South Dakota is a *very* important state," Mrs. H. said. "Does anyone want to take a *guess* about the capital?"

Belzer raised his hand. "Is it France?"

Mrs. Heinie shook her head. "Come on, people. You know this. The capital of South Dakota?"

Belzer raised his hand again. "Is it *North* Dakota?"

"Are you trying to be funny?" Mrs. Heinie asked him.

Belzer squinted at her. "Funny?"

"I'm a little surprised at you all," Mrs. Heinie said. "You were supposed to study your capitals last night. I—"

She suddenly stopped. She saw that no one was listening.

A lot of kids had turned to the window and were staring out.

What were they gawking at?

I jumped out of my seat so I could see. "OH, NO!" I let out a horrified cry.

Gassy!

He had escaped from the dorm. The fat bulldog stood outside the classroom window, staring in. *And he had the lunchroom lady's WOODEN LEG between his teeth!*

Kids were pointing and screaming. A bunch of them ran to the window to get a better view.

I sank back into my seat and shut my eyes.

"Whose dog is that?" Mrs. Heinie demanded. "Does anyone know? Whose dog is that?"

And then I heard Sherman Oaks's voice ring out loud and clear: "It's Bernie's. It's Bernie's dog!"

I'm a Rotten Student

SAVE TREES

DON'T DO HOMEWORK!

I L♥ve my ROTTEN SCHOOL

It wasn't me! It was the dog!

Chapter 10

KIDNAPPED!

Mrs. Heinie pulled me aside. "Is that your dog, Bernie?"

"Dog? What dog?" I replied. "I didn't see a dog."

She stared at me through her thick glasses. "Bernie, even I saw that bulldog with the leg in his mouth! If you have a pet on campus, I have to report you to Headmaster Upchuck."

I raised my hands in surrender. "Mrs. Heinie," I said, "you caught me. I confess. I have sixteen Chihuahuas, two ducks, and a grizzly bear in my room."

"No jokes," she said. "Tonight, I'll be in your room for our nightly Good Night Handshake. And I'm going to search your room from top to bottom."

The Good Night Handshake is an old Rotten School tradition. It happens every night in all the dorms before Lights-Out.

In our dorm, Mrs. Heinie comes around at nine o'clock. She goes from room to room and checks everyone in for the night.

Then she asks each one of us, "How was your day? Did you have a good day?" And she shakes hands with each of us.

It's kind of nice to end each day with a handshake. But *not* if you're hiding a parrot and a bulldog in your room.

Mrs. H. squinted at me through her glasses. "If you have a pet in there, I'll find it," she said.

"I'll help you," I said. "If anyone is hiding pets in the dorm, we'll catch them—won't we!"

A few minutes later, I was crossing the Great Lawn, hurrying back to Rotten House. I walked with my head down, my shoulders hunched. Thinking hard.

Mrs. H. would be in my room tonight, searching every corner. No way I could hide Gassy and Lippy from her. I was doomed.

The afternoon sun was sinking behind the trees. Long shadows fell over the grass.

I saw Sherman Oaks across the lawn. The evil Sherman. He'd do anything to get me in trouble.

He wore his ostrich-skin backpack. And he was carrying something on his shoulder. A laundry bag?

Why would Sherman be carrying a bulging laundry bag across the Great Lawn?

I decided to follow him. Sherman was grunting and groaning. He started to stagger. The bag was heavy.

I kept in the shadows. I crept closer. Closer...

"Ohhhh, yuck." A disgusting smell washed over me.

I pinched my fingers over my nose. But it didn't help.

Gassy!

Sherman wasn't hauling a laundry bag. He was carrying my pet! Sherman had *kidnapped* my bulldog!

Where was Sherman taking him? Three guesses.

I stayed in the shadows. I moved behind the trees. I followed Sherman to Headmaster Upchuck's house.

He planned to rat me out. Sherman was about to show my dog to the Headmaster. And then it would be time to say, "Bye-bye, Bernie." I'd be on the next bus home.

Nice guy, huh?

I watched Sherman lower Gassy to the ground. He had the dog on a leash. He tied the leash to a slender tree next to the Headmaster's house.

Then Sherman walked up to the front door and rang the bell.

I had to act fast. If Headmaster Upchuck came out and saw Gassy, it was all over.

But what could I do?

Chapter 11

MEOW

Think fast. Think fast, Bernie.

Turning, I saw Belzer strolling across the grass. I waved to him. "Belzer—get over here! Hurry!"

Belzer bounced over to me, his stomach bumping up and down under his T-shirt. "What's up, Big B?" he asked.

"Shhh. No time to explain," I said. I pulled Belzer over to Gassy. When he saw me, the dog's stubby tail started wagging like crazy. Gassy knew I was going to rescue him.

I tugged the leash off Gassy. I gave him a gentle

slap on the butt, and Gassy trotted away.

Then I slid the leash over Belzer's neck. "Quick. Sit," I said.

Belzer sat down in the grass with the leash around his neck.

"Good boy," I said. I petted him on the head. "When Headmaster Upchuck comes out, here's what you say: *'He tied me up! Sherman tied me up.'* Get it?"

"Got it, Big B," Belzer said. He flashed me a thumbs-up. "How long do I have to wear this leash?"

No time to answer. The door to the Headmaster's house swung open. Sherman started to pull Headmaster Upchuck to the tree.

The Headmaster is a tiny man, about the same height as us fourth graders. He wears the same gray suit every day. I think he took it off a ventriloquist's dummy.

I darted behind a nearby bush. Then I peeked out and watched.

Sherman looked very excited. He had a big smile on his face. "I have proof that Bernie Bridges has a pet at school," he told the Headmaster. "Here it is— Bernie's dog."

Headmaster Upchuck stared down at Belzer. Belzer sat on the grass, looking sad. He tugged at the tight leash around his neck. "He tied me up!" Belzer cried. "Sherman tied me up!"

Sherman's mouth dropped open. His eyes bulged.

Headmaster Upchuck scowled at him. "Is this some kind of a joke?" he growled. "You know I don't have a sense of humor. I don't get jokes."

"But—but—but—" Sherman sputtered.

"Untie Belzer," Headmaster Upchuck ordered. "We have a school rule against tying up other students."

"Yes, sir," Sherman said weakly. He slid the leash off Belzer. Belzer rubbed his neck.

And just at that moment, a sound came out of Sherman's backpack. A very loud *meee-oww*.

"What was that?" Headmaster Upchuck demanded.

"Uh…nothing," Sherman answered.

"It sounded like a cat," Belzer said.

Another loud *meee-oww* poured out of the back-pack.

"Sherman Oaks, are you hiding a pet?" the Headmaster asked. "Open your backpack. At once."

Sherman sighed and pulled off his backpack. He unzipped it and pulled out his metal cat.

The cat *meowed*, dropped to the grass, and clawed at Headmaster Upchuck's pants leg with both paws.

"He tore my pants!" Headmaster Upchuck cried. "Get him off me! He's shredding my pants!"

Sherman struggled to pull the cat away. But he couldn't tear the cat off the Headmaster's pants.

Belzer found me behind the bush. We took off, trotting toward Rotten House.

An awesome afternoon.

Behind us, I could hear Headmaster Upchuck screaming at Sherman. "Shut that thing off! Shut it off—and give me the batteries!"

Score one for Bernie B.

"Look what fell out of Sherman's backpack," Belzer said. He handed me a wad of raffle tickets.

"Oh, wow. These are the ten tickets I sold him," I said. "Terrific. I'll sell them to him again. At *twice* the price!" I shoved them into my pocket.

I felt good. But I knew the pet war wasn't over. I knew Sherman wouldn't give up.

And Mrs. Heinie would be in my room tonight. My sweet pets weren't safe.

---- Chapter 12 ----

DOOMED!

At dinner in the Dining Hall, I ate my food and Belzer's, too. Being brilliant takes a lot of energy.

After dinner most of the guys went to their rooms to do homework. Feenman, Crench, and I studied, too. We studied some PlayStation games in the Common Room.

When I glanced at the clock, it was nearly nine. Oh, wow. Nearly nine. And I realized I was DOOMED.

I heard Mrs. Heinie come downstairs. It was time for nine o'clock Lights-Out—*and the Good Night handshake.*

I hurried to my room. I covered Lippy's perch. *"BEAK me!"* he squawked. *"Beak me!"*

But he settled down after a few seconds.

I hoisted Gassy onto the bed and slid him under the covers. "Don't move a muscle," I told him.

"*Shut your BEAK!*" Lippy called.

I threw a dozen or so T-shirts over his stand to muffle the sound.

I sat down on the bed and tried to cover the big lump. Could I get away with it? Through my open door, I saw Mrs. Heinie in the other room. She was shaking hands with Feenman. "Good night, Mrs. Heinie," Feenman said. She shook hands with Crench and Belzer.

"Put the balloons away," she told Crench. "You can make more funny noises tomorrow."

PPHHHHRRRRAAAAAT.

The three guys giggled like madmen.

Mrs. H. turned and headed into my room.

This was it. The big test.

"Hello, Mrs. H.," I said. "Beautiful night, isn't it?"

"*Shut your BEAK!*" Lippy squawked. Lippy's voice was muffled, but she could still hear him.

Mrs. Heinie squinted at me through her glasses. "What did you say?"

"I said, come take a PEEK."

"That's what I plan to do," Mrs. Heinie said, gazing around.

"Eat FEATHERS!"

Lippy squawked from his cage.

"Bernie, what did you say?" Mrs. H. repeated.

"I said, lovely WEATHER."

Mrs. Heinie began searching my room for pets. She sniffed around in every corner. She searched my closet. She went through my dresser drawers. She even got down on her knees and searched under my bed. "I don't like that smile on your face, Bernie," she said. "I know you're hiding pets in here somewhere."

"I'm only smiling because I'm happy to see you," I said. I flashed her my best dimples. "You bring a little sunshine to all of us boys, Mrs. H."

"Cut the baloney," she said. She sighed. "I can't find any animals. Guess I'll say good night."

She started to shake my hand—then stopped.

Her eyes bulged, and her mouth dropped open.

She was staring at the bed. Staring because Gassy had poked his head up through the covers. Gassy had his head on the pillow, staring up at Mrs. H.

"Uh…I can explain this," I said.

Chapter 13

THE NEW STUDENT

Think fast, Bernie. Think fast.

"Mrs. Heinie, have you met the new student?" I said.

She blinked several times. "New student?"

"Yes. He arrived today. Meet...uh...Barry Bone."

Mrs. Heinie squinted at Gassy. "Welcome to Rotten House."

Gassy burped.

Mrs. Heinie turned to me. "I'm shocked. I don't believe you're *sharing* your room! You never wanted a roommate. You always wanted to be by yourself."

71

"Oh. Well...I wanted to give the new kid a break," I said. "You know. Help him get a good start."

"That's so nice of you, Bernie," Mrs. Heinie said.

A big gob of drool ran down Gassy's chin. I stepped behind him and hugged him to cover the drool.

"Bernie—what are you doing?" Mrs. Heinie asked.

"I'm starting a *new* tradition," I told her. "A nightly handshake *and* a nightly hug." I tightened my hug around Gassy.

Mrs. Heinie had a tear in one eye. "Bernie, I never knew you had such a sweet side. A nightly hug is a wonderful idea."

She stepped forward and stuck out her hand. "Barry, welcome to Rotten House. We shake hands every night."

I still had a tight hug around the dog's middle. I stuck out my hand, and she shook it.

"And good night to you, too, Bernie," she said. I stuck out my hand again, and she shook it again.

Mrs. Heinie turned and headed out the door.

72

Yaay. Talk about a close one!

As soon as Mrs. Heinie was gone, Feenman, Belzer, and Crench hurried into my room.

"Bernie, she almost caught you," Feenman said. "That new student idea was brilliant."

"Brilliant!" Belzer repeated.

"But she'll catch on," Crench said. "What are you going to do?"

"No problem. We'll do it right," I said. "We'll enroll Barry in school."

Chapter 14

JELLY BEANS

I listened until Mrs. H. climbed the stairs to her apartment in the attic. I heard her door close. Then Feenman, Crench, and I got dressed and tiptoed out of the dorm.

It was a cool, breezy night. Very dark. No moon or stars.

Our sneakers slid over the wet grass. I was in a hurry. Feenman and Crench had to jog to keep up with me.

"Tell me again, Bernie," Feenman whispered. "Why are we sneaking into the Headmaster's office?"

"To enroll the new student," I said.

We made our way to Upchuck's building. He was asleep. All the lights were out upstairs.

We sneaked in through a back window. Our flashlights danced over the walls. The Headmaster had a big desk, cluttered with papers and files. A desktop computer sat at one side.

On the wall, I saw two framed photographs. One was of Headmaster Upchuck in a black graduation robe. The other showed him at some theme park, shaking hands with SpongeBob SquarePants.

Weird.

"Hey, check it out," Crench whispered. "He keeps a jar of jelly beans on his desk." Crench pulled off the lid and helped himself.

Feenman grabbed a few from the jar. "Yo, Crench. What's your favorite flavor?"

"Cucumber," Crench said. "I love the cucumber ones."

"I like the white ones that have no flavor at all," Feenman said. "Those are awesome!"

"We're not here for jelly beans," I said. "This is serious. Did you forget?"

76

Feenman and Crench swallowed. "What do we do, Bernie?"

"Go through that stack of papers," I said, beaming my light on the desk. "Find the 'New Student file.'"

They began pawing through the stack. I moved to the file cabinets against the wall and began to search.

"Found it!" I whispered, pulling out a thick file. "Okay, dudes. We're in business."

I spread the file out on the desktop. "Here we go. Registration form. Keep your light on it. Hey, Crench—what are you doing?"

"I got a green onion one," he said. "Awesome." He tossed a few more jelly beans into his mouth. "Mmmm. Tomato."

I pulled out my pen and leaned over the registration form.

"Hey, Bernie, what's up with this? How is this going to work?" Feenman asked.

"I enroll Gassy as a transfer student," I said. "If Gassy is a student, he can't be a pet—right? And if he's not a pet, I can't be kicked out of school."

"But—but—" Feenman stammered. "It won't work. It *can't* work."

"Take it easy," I said. "He won't be the *only* student in this school who walks on all fours!"

Crench was grabbing for the jelly beans again. He was no help at all. But Feenman held his flashlight over the New Student form. And I filled it out.

I wrote Gassy's new name on the form: BARRY A. BONE. Then I scribbled stuff over the rest of the page.

"I'm so proud. Barry's gonna be a Rotten Student!" I said. "Crench—get away from the jelly beans. Open that supply closet over there. Find Barry a school T-shirt and a cap."

Crench opened the closet and began to search through the shelves of shirts and sweatshirts. "Problem, Bernie," he said. "They don't have dog sizes."

"Never mind that," I said. "Just get a large."

He handed me a shirt and a cap. "Better get me *two* shirts," I said. "Barry spits up a lot."

Crench handed me another shirt.

"Okay. We're done. Let's get out of here," I said.

"I've got to get Barry ready for school tomorrow."

We started to the door. But Crench just couldn't resist. He saw two dark beans resting on the desk. He picked them up and popped them into his mouth. He chewed for a moment. Then he made a disgusted face. "Sick. These taste *awful*."

"That's because they're not jelly beans," I said. "That was mouse poop."

Chapter 15

First-Day Jitters

The next morning, Belzer walked Barry while I ate breakfast. I could barely swallow my bacon, sausage, hash browns, cheese Danish, and hominy grits. I was nervous about Barry's first day in class.

When Belzer returned, I told him to get the new student dressed for school.

It wasn't easy.

Belzer had a hard time pulling the shirt over Barry's head and down his legs. Barry kept growling and snapping at him.

"Ow. My arm. I'm bleeding!" Belzer cried. "Look

what that dog did to me. I'm bleeding!"

"It's only a flesh wound," I said. "Be a man, Belzer! The new student is just a little nervous on his first day."

"It isn't going to work if he bites everyone!" Belzer said.

"They'll just think he's friendly," I said.

Belzer finally finished with the shirt. Then he tucked the baseball cap over Barry's floppy bulldog ears. "Listen to me. It isn't going to work, Big B," Belzer said. "Look. He's drooling on his shirt."

"So does Feenman," I said. "Let's go. It's almost time for class."

We led Barry downstairs. We were almost out the door when we ran into Billy the Brain. "Hey, what's up, guys?" he greeted us.

"Just heading to class," I said. "Why the big smile, dude?"

"Check this out," he said. He flashed a paper in front of me. "I aced the History test, Bernie. I got a forty-eight. Believe it?"

"Wow." I stared at his test paper. He got almost *half* the questions right! "Good work, Billy," I said.

"Whoa, dude. That will bring up the curve for the whole class."

He turned to Barry. "Hey—how's it going?" he asked the dog.

Barry stared up at him with his runny brown eyes.

"Transfer student," I told Billy. "First day."

"Hey, good luck," Billy said. He reached out his right hand to shake hands with Barry.

"Shake," I whispered. "Shake."

Barry raised a paw. They shook hands. Billy hurried off.

As soon as he was gone, Belzer turned to me. "Bernie—he didn't even notice. Did you see? Billy the Brain didn't even notice that Barry is a dog!"

I scratched my chin. "Maybe we need to think of a new nickname for Billy," I said.

Belzer nodded. "You mean, like, Billy the Moron?"

"No time for that now," I said. I gave Barry a shove out the door. "Let's see if we can fool everyone else. If we can't, I'm in deep trouble."

A few minutes later, I walked Barry into Mrs. Heinie's classroom. "Mrs. H.," I called. "Here is the new transfer student. Barry Bone. Where should he sit?"

I heard a loud *BRAAAAAT*.

Mrs. Heinie turned around. She wrinkled up her nose. "OOH. What's that smell?" she gasped. "What's that horrible STINK?"

Kids pinched their fingers over their noses. The classroom filled with moans and groans.

Barry stared up at Mrs. Heinie, and she stared back at him.

My legs started to tremble. Would she see that her new student looked a lot like a bulldog?

Chapter 16

HE SPEAKS FRENCH

The loudspeaker squealed on.

ANNOUNCEMENTS

We heard Headmaster Upchuck clear his throat. "Attention, students," he said. "Many of you have requested that we use only *one*-letter words in the Spelling Bee. We have decided that might be too easy. So, the Spelling Bee is canceled. The Smelling Bee is also canceled."

Mrs. Heinie stared at my fat bulldog. "Barry, we were just about to start our French lessons," she said. "Do you speak any French?"

Barry let out a burp.

Burp!

"What did he say?" Mrs. Heinie asked. "I couldn't hear."

"He said, '*Oui, Madame,*'" I replied. "He's very shy. He speaks very quietly."

Mrs. Heinie smiled at Barry. "How many years of French have you had?" she asked.

Barry burped again. Some drool dripped down his chin.

"He said, '*Trois ans*,'" I told her.

"Wow. Three years of French! You're way ahead of our class," Mrs. H. said. "I'm impressed."

Barry was off to a good start.

"Have a seat, Barry," Mrs. Heinie said.

"He'll sit next to me," I said. I bumped Feenman out of his chair and motioned for Barry to jump up.

Mrs. Heinie squinted at the dog through her thick glasses. "Let's start our French lesson now. Barry, you can let us know if we're saying everything correctly."

Barry burped up some of his breakfast. I mopped it up and helped him into his chair.

The rest of the morning went very smoothly. Barry sat at his desk and stared alertly at Mrs. Heinie with his tongue hanging out. Luckily, three or four other students had their tongues hanging out.

I relaxed a little bit. I didn't have to worry—until choir practice.

Chapter 17

HE SINGS, TOO

Mr. Buzz Off is our music teacher. Mr. Off works us really hard. He's really proud of the fourth-grade choir, and he wants us to be perfect.

He makes us sing the same song over and over. And he sings right along with us. The funny thing is, Mr. Off is a terrible singer. He can't carry a tune.

It's a school joke to say he sings a little *off*. Ha-ha.

Well, I didn't think Barry was Mr. Off's kind of singer. So I shuffled sideways into the music room, trying to hide Barry behind me.

But Barry didn't stay hidden. He walked out from between my legs.

"Ah, the new student!" Mr. Off said. "Welcome. Don't hide. I'm sure you have a lovely voice."

Barry had soaked the front of his T-shirt with drool. But he managed to keep his cap on over his ears.

"Let's give you a tryout to see where you should sit," Mr. Off told Barry.

Uh-oh. My heart started to do flip-flops. A tryout?

"He has a very sore throat, sir," I said, stepping in front of Barry. "See? He can barely speak."

Barry let out a soft wheeze.

"Well, let's try singing something simple, then," Mr. Off said. He lowered his face to Barry. "Do you know the Overture to Beethoven's *Requiem* in D?"

"Yes. That's his favorite, sir," I said, again trying to block the dog from view. "But his throat...I'm afraid it's strep, sir. He's been coughing all morning."

"Bernie, give him a chance," Mr. Off said. "I see he's very shy. But he needs to try out for our choir."

I'm doomed, I realized. I'm busted. It's all over. I'll be out of here and home tomorrow night.

91

"Barry, let's first try something easy. Just sing along with me," Mr. Off said. He opened his mouth, shut his eyes, and began belting out a blues song.

He sang at the top of his voice. And his singing was so bad—so *off*—that Barry started to howl.

Barry tilted his head back and howled and howled.

Mr. Off stopped singing. He stared at Barry.

This is the end, I realized. *My final seconds in this school.*

"Very bluesy," Mr. Off told Barry. "You've got *soul!*"

I started to breathe again.

"And you have a lovely tenor voice," Mr. Off told Barry. "Go sit on the end over there. I'm going to make you *lead* tenor."

Oh, wow. You *go*, dog!

Barry was a hit. His first morning—and he was our best French student *and* the lead tenor of our choir.

After school I walked Barry back to the dorm. Belzer followed along, carrying my books. I slapped him a high five.

"We've got it made!" I said. "Barry is the perfect Rotten School Student. Am I brilliant or am I just brilliant?"

"You're brilliant, Big B," Belzer agreed.

A great day. I felt good all evening.

Until Mrs. Heinie came in at nine for the Good Night Handshake.

"Don't forget, guys. Tomorrow is school testing day," she said. "So get plenty of sleep. Remember? It's a six-hour test."

She turned and walked away.

I sat shivering in my bed. A six-hour test?

Barry licked my face. The poor guy didn't realize he was about to flunk out of school—and take me with him.

Chapter 18

BARRY'S FIRST EXAM

I woke up the next morning, heavy with gloom.

A six-hour test. The entire school was taking the annual Achievement test. No way Barry could pass. No way Barry could *sit* through it.

I stared down at him. The cute guy wagged his stubby tail and grinned at me. I patted his head. Then I pulled his cap over his ears.

I let out a long, sad sigh. "Let's go, boy," I said. "Time for your first—and last—exam."

The dining hall was already packed with kids when Barry and I walked in. All the classes were taking the exam—second graders through eighth graders.

Barry and I took seats at a table near the back. Three teachers were passing out test booklets and pencils. I took Barry's test booklet for him and set it down on his desk.

I started to show him how to mark the little boxes on the answer sheet. But Barry snapped his teeth around the pencil and started chewing.

Hopeless. It was hopeless.

The bell rang. "Okay, Rotten Students," one of the teachers said, "you may begin your exams. Good luck to you all."

Yeah, good luck. I was going to need a lot more than good luck this morning. I gazed at Barry. He had a puddle of drool on his test booklet.

I opened it for him, shoved the pencil into his paw, and started his paw moving over the answers. Then I opened my test, lowered my head, and went to work.

The big room grew silent. I answered the questions on three or four pages without looking up. The test was pretty easy.

Down the table, I saw April-May June. She raised

her beautiful head. She sniffed the air with her perfect, turned-up nose. Then she let out a cry. "Ooh—what's that smell?"

Moans and groans and cries spread around the room.

"What STINKS? Something STINKS!"

"Eeeuuu! I can't stand it! What's that smell?"

"Rotten eggs? Dead fish? Burning rubber?"

"Ohhhhhh, help. I'm sick! It's making me SICK!"

Kids had tears running down their faces. Some were choking and gagging. The sound of loud vomiting echoed off the high ceiling.

Once again, Gassy was showing off his main talent.

And now the stampede was on.

Groaning and crying and holding their noses, kids pushed out the door. Test booklets flew to the floor as kids leaped up and fled from the Dining Hall.

In seconds, the big room was empty.

I couldn't stand the smell, either. I closed my test booklet and ran out the door. "Well," I told myself, "that went well, didn't it!"

Chapter 19

THE LUCKY WINNER

The next morning, Barry and I took our seats near the back of the class. I saw right away that Mrs. Heinie had a serious look on her face.

The bell rang. Mrs. Heinie raised her hands to get everyone quiet. "People. People, may I have your attention? Headmaster Upchuck will be here in a moment to talk about yesterday's exam."

Uh-oh.

The exam really had turned into a SMELLING Bee! And it was all my fault. Mine and Barry's, I mean.

I started practicing my good-bye speech.

Next to me, Barry started panting really loudly. Then, before I could stop him, he jumped down from his chair. I made a grab for him, but he got away.

The dog's cap flew off, and he went running to Mrs. Heinie at the front of the class. "Barry—come back!" I called. "No—please!"

Too late.

Barry jumped up on Mrs. Heinie and wrapped his front paws around her leg.

"Get off me!" Mrs. Heinie screamed. She started twisting and kicking. Her glasses went flying.

Sherman jumped up from his seat. "He's a DOG!" Sherman cried. "He's not a boy. He's a DOG!"

"Get him OFF me!" Mrs. Heinie shrieked.

I flew to the front of the class and tried to pull Gassy off Mrs. Heinie's leg. That's when Headmaster Upchuck entered the room.

He let out a loud gasp. "What is going *on* here?" he demanded.

I pulled Gassy off Mrs. Heinie's leg and held the panting cutie tightly in both hands.

"You're looking very sharp today, sir," I said to Headmaster Upchuck. "Now, what movie star do you remind me of? Is it Tom Cruise? I love that button-down shirt. They have such nice bargains in the kids' department, don't they!"

The headmaster ignored me. He stared at Gassy. "That's a dog," he said. "What is a dog doing in the classroom?"

"It's Bernie's!" Sherman cried.

Mrs. Heinie rubbed her leg. "The new student is a dog, Headmaster Upchuck. Barry A. Bone is a dog!"

The Headmaster thought about it for a moment. Then a big smile spread over his face. "Pets are not allowed in school," he said. "That means I get to kick Bernie Bridges out. I get to send Bernie Bridges home!"

He started to laugh. He tossed back his head and laughed till tears ran down his face. He did a little dance, his tiny shoes tapping the floor. "This is the happiest day of my life!" Headmaster Upchuck cried.

"But this isn't my dog!" I cried. "I can prove it!"

The Headmaster's smile vanished. "Not your dog?

Then whose is it?"

"I'll let you know in five minutes," I said.

He scowled at me.

"Just give me five minutes, sir," I said.

He nodded. "Okay. Five minutes. Your *last* five minutes in this school! I'll say good-bye to you in my office!" He turned and walked out.

Feenman hurried over to me. "Bernie, what are you doing?" he asked.

"I just thought of the grand prize for the raffle," I told him. "It's Gassy! The winner gets Gassy."

"But, Bernie—" Feenman started.

"Don't you see?" I said, putting my hand over his mouth. "The winner will own Gassy. That means Gassy won't be *my* pet any longer. So I won't get kicked out of school."

"How can you give Gassy away?" Feenman asked. "You *love* that dog."

"It'll all blow over," I said. "Don't worry. I'll get him back."

I ran to the front of the class. "Okay, everyone— get out your raffle tickets!" I said. "I'm going to draw the winning ticket now."

I pulled the stubs from my backpack. Kids were pulling out their raffle tickets. Sherman was searching his backpack, looking for his tickets.

"Check your number, everyone," I shouted. "The winner gets a beautiful bulldog! A bulldog of your very own!"

I picked the winning ticket stub. "Here is the grand prize winner," I said. "It's ticket number 32489. Who has it? Check your tickets. Who wins the dog? Who has number 32489?"

Silence. No one answered.

"Dudes, come on," I said, checking my watch. "Who has the winning ticket?"

"Bernie—check your pocket," Belzer whispered.

My pocket? Oh, right.

I pulled out the ten tickets that had fallen out of Sherman's backpack. Now they were mine. And there it was right on top—ticket number 32489.

I stared at the ticket. I gulped. I blinked. "I—I won the dog," I stammered. "*I'm* the…(sob)…lucky winner!"

The kids began to boo and hiss. They thought the raffle was a cheat.

Mrs. Heinie came running up to me. "Then the dog is yours, after all," she said. She grabbed my arm. "Come with me, Bernie. I'm very sorry. But rules are rules. We'll all miss you here at the Rotten School."

Chapter 20

THE HONOR STUDENT

Mrs. Heinie dragged me to Headmaster Upchuck's office. "The dog belongs to Bernie," she told him.

"Sweet!" Headmaster Upchuck cried happily. He pumped his tiny fists in the air. "Yes! Yes! I can send you home! Sweet!"

Then he froze. "Oh. Wait a minute." He opened the big folder in his hand. He started to study it. "Oh, wait," he said. "Oh, no. Oh, no."

His shoulders slumped. He let out a long sigh.

He turned to Mrs. Heinie. "Barry A. Bone was the only student who stayed for the whole exam yesterday," he said. "He got the highest score on the test."

Mrs. Heinie's mouth dropped open. She stared at Headmaster Upchuck. "You mean—?"

"The dog is on the Honor Roll," Upchuck said. "I can't send him away. The school average will go down too low."

Mrs. Heinie started to stutter. "B-B-Bernie's d-dog—he gets to stay in school?"

The Headmaster nodded. "Yes. He's our top student. He'll have to stay. I'll change the rule immediately. Pets *are* allowed at the Rotten School."

I sang out a loud cheer of victory as Barry trotted into the room. "Thank you, sir," I said, shaking Upchuck's hand. "You won't regret this. Barry will be a credit to the school, sir. Barry will make you proud."

"HELP!" Mrs. Heinie cried. "Get him off me! Get the new student off my LEG!"

The Good, the Bad
and the Very Slimy

BELZER HAS A PROBLEM

You are probably wondering why I, Bernie Bridges, decided to change my behavior, change my personality, and become a whole new person.

A *new* Bernie Bridges! It's a frightening thought—isn't it?

Especially since the *old* Bernie Bridges was *perfect*!

Well, the new Bernie Bridges had to be even perfecter. You'll see why...

Don't get me wrong. I think life is perfect here at the Rotten School. I think all kids should go to boarding school and live away from home.

My buddies and I live in an old house at the back of the campus, called Rotten House. No parents! It's a great life.

Of course, we do have some problems with those goody-goody kids who live in the dorm across from us. It's called Nyce House. What kind of geek would live in a place called *Nyce* House?

But I'm getting away from my story. And I know you're very eager to hear my story—since it's all about *me*...

It started one night after dinner in the Student Center. That's where my guys and I go every night to shoot some pool, play video games, and hang out.

I was walking through the game room when I heard my friend Belzer shouting to me.

"Bernie, my hand is stuck! Help me! I'm *stuck!*"

Why do my friends always call *me* when they're in trouble? Is it because they know I'm a genius?

"Bernie—help me!"

It didn't take me long to see the problem. Belzer was crunched down on his knees. His hand was stuck in the candy bar vending machine. Actually, his *whole arm* was stuck inside the slot.

He turned to me. He had sweat pouring down his chubby face. The poor guy was in pain. "Big B—get me *outta* this!"

I rested my hand on his head. "Belzer, how many times do I have to tell you? *First*, you put the money in the machine. *Then* you reach for the candy bar. You always do it backwards."

"But, Bernie, you *took* all my money—remember?" Belzer whined. "You said you were starting a college fund for me."

"You're nine years old," I said. "You have to start thinking about the future. I put the money in a safe place for you."

"A safe place?"

"Yes. My wallet."

I tugged his shoulder. He let out a cry. The poor guy was really stuck.

"Better start getting used to your new nickname," I said.

Belzer gazed up at me with those big, wet cow eyes of his. "New nickname?"

"Yes. *One-Arm*. It's kinda catchy, don't you think?"

4

ABOUT THE AUTHOR

photo by Dan Nelken

R.L. Stine graduated from the Rotten School with a solid D+ average, which put him at the top of his class. He says that his favorite activities at school were Scratching Body Parts and Making Armpit Noises.

In sixth grade, R.L. won the school Athletic Award for his performance in the Wedgie Championships. Unfortunately, after the tournament, his underpants had to be surgically removed.

R.L. was very popular in school. He could tell this because kids always clapped and cheered whenever he left the room. One of his teachers remembers him fondly: "R.L. was a hard worker. He was so proud of himself when he learned to wave bye-bye with both hands."

After graduation, R.L. became well known for writing scary book series such as The Nightmare Room, Fear Street, Goosebumps, and Mostly Ghostly, and a short story collection called *Beware!*

Today, R.L. lives in a cage in New York City, where he is busy writing stories about his school days. Says he: "I wish everyone could be a Rotten Student."

For more information
about R.L. Stine,
go to www.rottenschool.com
and www.rlstine.com

ROTTEN SCHOOL